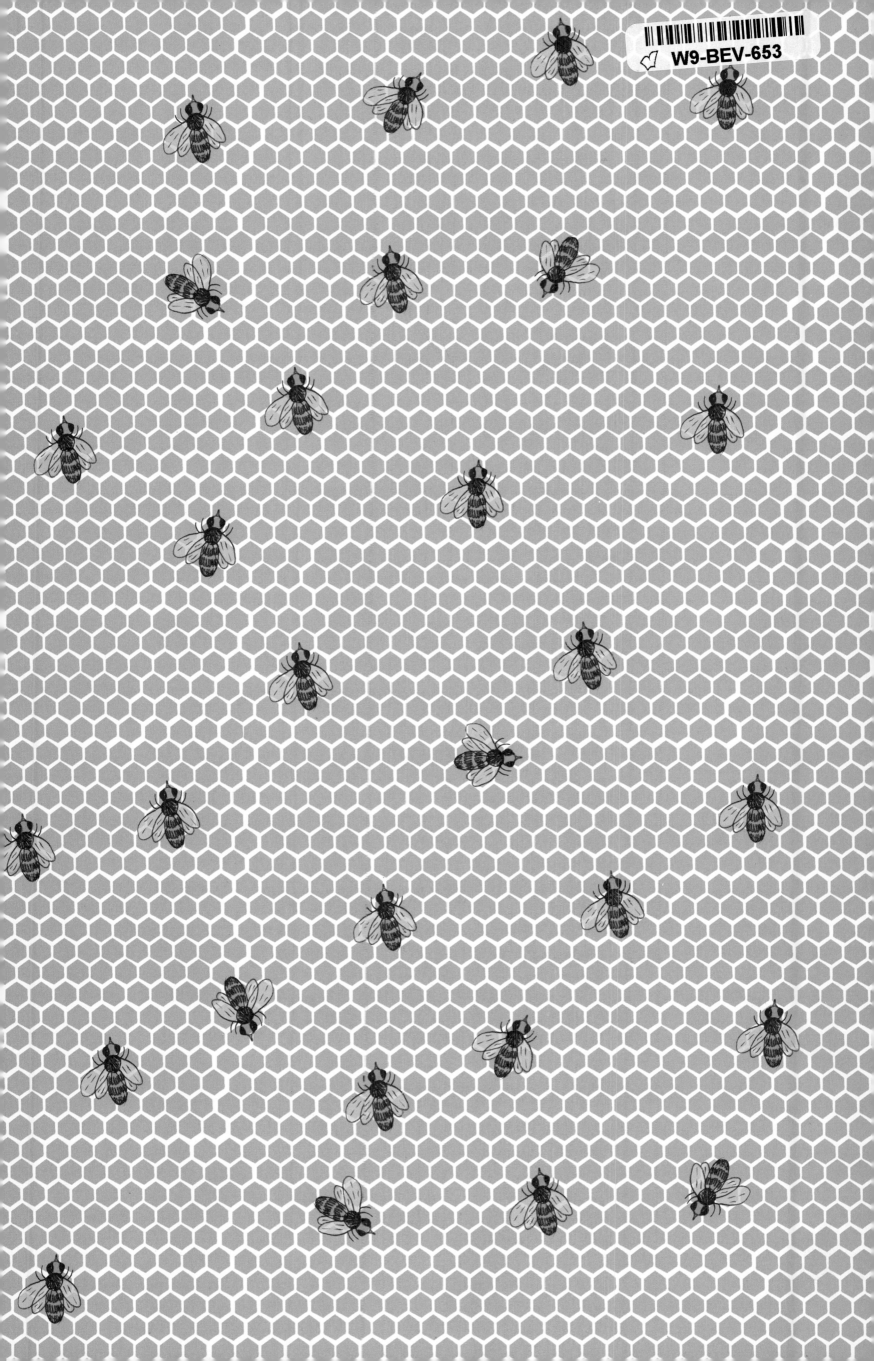

For Matyash

First published in the United States in 2013 by
Chronicle Books LLC.

First published in France in 2011 under the title
Une chanson d'ours by hélium, 12, rue de l'Arbalète
75005 Paris.

Typeset in ClickClack.

Manufactured in China.

Library of Congress Cataloging-in-Publication
Data available.

ISBN: 978-1-4521-1424-8

10 9 8 7 6 5 4 3 2

Chronicle Books LLC
680 Second Street
San Francisco, California 94107

www.chroniclekids.com

the BEAR'S SONG

BENJAMIN CHAUD

chronicle books·san francisco

Deep in his den, Papa Bear starts to snore. Winter whistles through the forest. Hibernation has begun.

But Little Bear is too caught up in honey thoughts to hear winter's whisper. A busy sort of buzzing beckons him instead.

Papa Bear wakes with a start. "Where did my Little Bear run off to now?" he wonders.

With a bounce and a bound, Papa Bear dashes through the trees.
He searches every corner of the forest, but he just can't find his cub.

Papa Bear has run so far from the forest that he is now surrounded
by the noise and smoke of the big city.

But through the crowd, Papa Bear catches sight of two fuzzy ears.
Could they belong to Little Bear?

Lost in the hustle and bustle, Papa Bear's heart sinks. But, wait!
Over there!

Papa Bear spies Little Bear racing after one frazzled-looking bee!

Papa Bear rushes through the opera house doors, knocks over a coatrack, and finds himself in a room gleaming from floor to ceiling.

Looking rather dapper indeed, Papa Bear darts across the hall.
Now where could that bee and that Little Bear be?

Papa Bear snuffles his snout through a backstage door, startling
a flock of strange, feathered birds who squawk as they scatter.

With no time to apologize, Papa Bear flees! Downstairs, then up,
toward the sweet sounds of music. Until . . .

... with a crash and a gasp, Papa Bear tumbles down to the stage!

Thank goodness for the great chandelier.

Oh. Never mind.
Blinded by light and frozen by fear, Papa Bear does not know what
to do. But then he gets an idea.

"Maybe I should sing the Bear's Song, a lullaby that all bears love." So Papa Bear clears his big bear throat, and opens his big bear mouth, and he starts to sing . . .

Wait a minute. Where is everyone going?

Were they frightened by Papa Bear's song?

Papa Bear's ears twitch at the sound of two paws clapping. "Bravo, Papa!" says Little Bear. "That was beautiful!"

"I have a surprise for you!" Little Bear explains, "I followed the bee, and you must see what I found!"

High up on the opera house roof, under the stars and among the beehives, Papa Bear and his cub settle in to sleep.

After all, hibernation is better with honey. And adventure is best
enjoyed together.

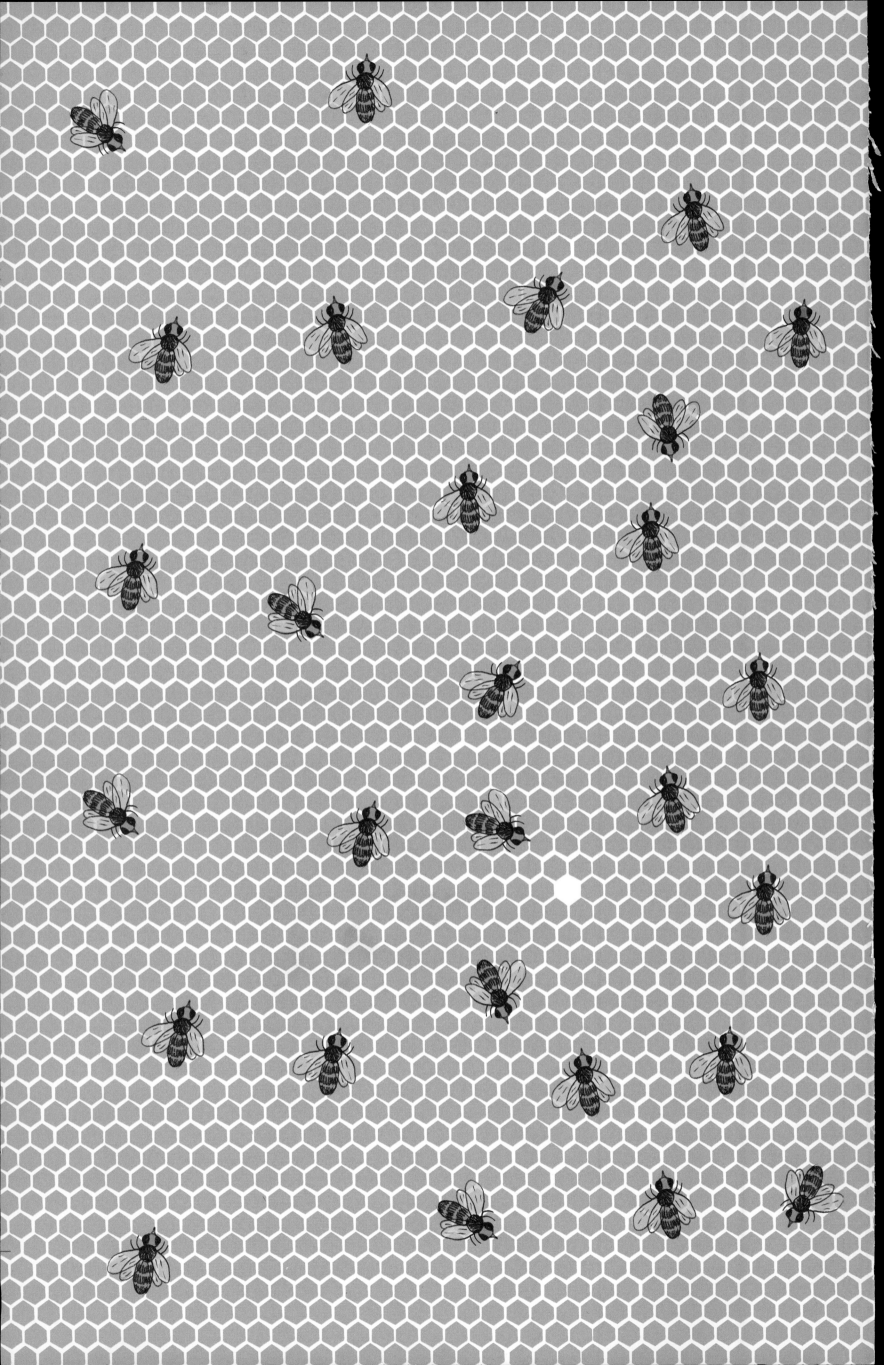